The Angel With a Mouth-Organ

To Carl Hollander and Astra Lacis
And to Osvalds Lacis and all the other fathers

The Angel
With a Mouth-Organ

Christobel Mattingley

illustrated by Astra Lacis

HOLIDAY HOUSE/NEW YORK

We had put the baubles, the tinsel, the lights on the Christmas tree. The angel was always last of all.

Peter and Ingrid started to argue and grab at its box.

"It's my turn!"

"You did it last year."

"I'm taller, so I can reach better."

"It's not fair!"

I said, "Hand piles!"

Peter put down his right hand. Ingrid put hers on top, I covered Ingrid's.

Peter covered mine and said, "Sorry, Mum".

Ingrid covered Peter's and said, "You will tell us the angel story again, won't you?"

Inside the box the little glass angel with the golden wing shone like a star against the cotton wool.

I thought of the baby doll wrapped ready for Ingrid to find on Christmas morning, and the baby growing in my tummy, which Peter hoped would be a brother.

It started the year I wanted a baby doll. I'd hoped for a real baby, like our neighbour had. My mother wouldn't promise. So I asked for a doll instead.

But long before St Nicholas could bring one, out of the clouds the planes came, with noise like thunder and flashes like lightning.

They flew across our village. It became a garden of flame. The houses and the haystacks were like poppies, bursting out of their buds into glowing gold and orange. The church spire and the chimneys were like spikes of scarlet salvia.

When all the petals of flame had fallen at last, the village was like a skeleton. Buildings were black, animals were dead, people had disappeared. The earth was bare and burnt. But in the hearts of the people who were left the fire flowers had dropped their seeds—of fear and of hate, of courage and of love.

After the planes the soldiers came. They took away fathers, brothers, sons. But they didn't take our father. He laughed, "They don't want a one-armed bear in their circus!" And he hugged us with the arm he had left, almost as hard as he used to hug when he had both arms, before the planes came.

My father found a cart and Mother packed it with all we had saved from our burning house—quilts and feather pillows, three cheeses and some sausages, onions and a pumpkin, a bag of flour, some pots and plates and cups and knives and spoons, her best cloth which my grandma had made, and the cuckoo clock.

My father had his mouth-organ in his pocket. My sister had her books in her school-bag. I had my doll with the golden hair in my arms. And our neighbour, whose husband had been taken by the soldiers, had her baby snug in a quilt-and-pillow nest in the cart beside Grandma.

Father put our cow into the shafts, Mother tied on a bucket and a bundle of singed hay, and we set off. Walking.

I didn't know where we were going . . .

how far we had to go. . .

when we would get there. . .

We walked and walked and walked. And always the sound of the thunder and the glow and the smell of the fire flowers were behind us.

We walked until the cow lay down and died, and many other people who were hungrier than we were, roasted her meat and made soup from her bones.

We walked until the baby died, and Father scratched a hole under a birch tree and my sister and I gathered moss for its new bed and leaves for its blankets. My sister tore a page from her school-book and wrote the baby's name. She slipped it under the stone our neighbour put on top of the leaves and earth.

We walked until our neighbour and our last cheese disappeared one night. Mother and Father didn't say anything. But Grandma, who now had the whole cart to herself, said, "It won't do her any good". Two days later I thought I saw someone wearing our neighbour's boots and I was sure I saw someone else wearing her shawl. But Mother and Father wouldn't say anything.

We walked until the sun grew thin and pale, and we grew thin and pale too. The days shrank into long cold nights and our flour bag shrank too. The leaves turned yellow and brown, wrinkled and brittle, and so did Grandma. My sister and I slept each side of her at night to keep her warm. But often we could hear her teeth chattering as she called to Grandpa in her dreams.

One morning there was an empty space between my sister and me. "She has gone to be with Grandpa," Mother said, as Father played Grandma's favourite tunes on his mouth-organ.

"Perhaps they're dancing now," my sister said. She took my hand and we danced the dances Grandma had taught us. Mother and Father danced too. Mother held Father's empty sleeve, because he needed his hand for his mouth-organ.

We walked until a wheel fell off our cart and before Father could mend it, some other people broke it up for firewood to roast an ox which had died. They didn't give us any. But Father said, "What would we be wanting with roast leather and burnt bones? And good riddance to the cart. We don't need it any longer. We'll get along faster without it".

He didn't say where we were getting along to. But we went on walking, each of us carrying a bundle which Mother had made out of the things left in the cart. I had the cups and the plates, and the spoons which rattled and the knives which poked me. My sister had the bucket with the pots in it. Mother had the food wrapped in Grandma's cloth. It wasn't a big bundle. Father had the quilts and the fat puffy pillows. He looked very funny. He sounded funny too, because the cuckoo in the clock would sometimes call from under the quilts, just as if it were at home beside the fireplace.

We walked and walked and sometimes the sound of thunder was very close. Then my father would play his mouth-organ. But even his merry tunes could not hide the smell of the fire flowers or drive away the smoke which made my sister cough and my eyes sting and run.

There were many people walking now and soldiers kept coming along in trucks, pushing us off the road. Then the roar of the planes was close and we could see them flying straight down the road towards us, with a spray of bullets blazing like lights on a Christmas tree.

My father pushed us into the ditch. Me and my doll. My sister on top. My mother on her. I felt the breath go out of me and my doll squeaked as Father threw himself across my mother. The cuckoo clock called, but I couldn't laugh because my mouth was full of doll's hair.

When my ears could properly hear again, the people sounds were shouts and curses. And when I could lift my face out of the mud, I could see all the walking people standing up and stretching and wiping the brown off themselves too. But many of the soldiers were lying still. There was red on their uniforms and no one could wipe it away.

My mother said, "Thank God they spared us". But the soldiers in the trucks were very angry. They took away all the men and the boys from the walking people. They took my father.

We did not know why they were taking him . . .
where they were taking him . . .
when we would see him again . . .

We went on walking and we came to a place where we didn't have to walk any further, because there were big huts where the walking people like us could stay. There were many more children than in our village and my sister took out her books and started a school. I liked playing mothers and fathers better. The boys only wanted to play soldiers.

They all joined in, though, when my sister and I sang our father's songs. And they organized some good gangs to scout along the railway lines and around the station for coal which had fallen from the trains. They always took my sister, because she had her bucket and because she was always brave. But after I cried when the guards shot one of my friends, they always tried to leave me behind even though I had torn the sleeves out of my blouse to try to stop him bleeding.

I was good at finding acorns, though. My father hadn't nicknamed me "Squirrel" for nothing. And I never cried when picking hips off the briars, no matter how sharp the thorns were.

That camp was starting to feel almost like home, when suddenly one day we had to move. This time we didn't walk. We were put on trains. There were different people at the new camp and we didn't see some of our friends again. But we made new friends and we joined a gang which looked for turnips and potatoes out in the fields at night. The toes of my boots had worn through and I had sores, but I loved the patterns of the frost crystals sparkling on the clods in the moonlight.

We always sang our father's songs with our mother before we went to sleep, and I was glad she still had two arms and could hold us tight at once. And if I woke in the dark with the sound of other peoples' nightmares, I would hum the tunes to myself and think about my father.

We were moved seven times. Birthdays and Christmases went by, without presents or parties, candles or cake, and always we wondered about Father. I lost my teeth one by one, and others came, but not very well. My sister grew tall, almost as tall as our mother. Our clothes were too small and our boots were worn out. We gathered leaves and grass and bark in the bucket to eat. And our mother's hair went grey.

The last time we were moved we went in cattle trucks. We didn't know where we were going. But the old thunder of planes and guns had been growing louder day by day and the smell of the fire flowers had been growing stronger.

The trucks were jammed with people and we children were glad when the train stopped at the edge of a wood and we were told to get off. We ran among the trees to play hide and seek and as I crouched against the trunk of a big fir tree, the planes came out of the clouds.

The bullets raked the train in long straight furrows, the way my father used to plough. And as I watched, the boiler on the engine began to spray in all directions, like a fountain in a park. It was one of the prettiest sights I had ever seen.

But the train couldn't go any more, so we clambered back into the trucks to fetch our belongings. The bullets had shredded my grandma's cloth as neat as coleslaw. And my doll had lost an arm.

We started to walk and I wondered where my father was and what he was doing. My sister started to sing his tunes. But I had a hard tight feeling in my chest and I couldn't sing. Then I heard a cuckoo call and I began to laugh. And I tied fir cones to my plaits and nodded my head and waved my arms and called, "Cuckoo! Cuckoo!"

I picked my mother a bunch of primroses and I didn't care if we couldn't eat them, because I was happy and I felt like flying.

We came to another camp which was even more crowded than the last, and in the huts there was no room for us or for the lady with the big tummy whom my mother had helped the last few days.

We had knocked on door after door, but the people all said, "Go away. There's no room for five more here. Go somewhere else".

We had tried almost every hut. It was growing dark and an icy little wind left over from winter was chasing us round every corner. Suddenly we saw a man open a shed door. He hurried in. My sister and I could tell he was important by his uniform. He jumped in to a car, looking very worried, and it drove away fast.

My sister and I ran into the shed. "It's empty," we called to our mother, quietly so that no one would hear. She came in with the lady and we closed the door softly. We smiled at each other in the half-dark. We had the whole place to ourselves and there were only four of us.

It was so quiet without the night noises of all the other people. Then the lady began making sounds we had heard before in the dark huts. My sister and I sang our father's songs out loud. Just before the light came again the baby was born and my mother wrapped it in the strips of linen that had been Grandma's cloth. I thought of the baby under the birch tree, and of my father, who could do almost as much with one hand as many people could do with two.

We all fell asleep then, but were woken quite soon when the sun was shining by the shouting outside.

"The war is over! The war is over!"

My mother jumped up and ran outside in her petticoat. My sister and I hugged each other and ran after her. The lady picked up her baby and followed us.

In the yard people were hugging and kissing, laughing and crying. Boys were whistling, girls were singing. Old women were crossing themselves and saying, "Thank God!" over and over again.

All day long the sun shone and people laughed and cheered, sang and danced. In the evening they pulled down fences and gates and guard posts and made a huge bonfire, and my sister and I went with the boys up to the village church on the hill. We rang and rang and rang the bell. And nobody stopped us.

The next day everything was different. Everyone wanted to go home. Everyone wanted to find their husband, their father, their sons, their brothers. People began leaving the camp and new people started moving in, trying to make their way home, looking for mothers, aunts, sisters, cousins.

"When shall we go to look for Father?" my sister and I asked our mother.

"Not yet," Mother said. "It's easier for one than three to travel. We'll wait here."

So after being walking people and talking people, we became waiting people. We waited while the searching people came and went, day by day, week by week.

And everyone asked each other, "Did you ever see . . . ?" and a thousand names and descriptions of big men, tall men, short women, stout women, naughty children, good children were exchanged and discussed. And people laughed or cried at the news they heard. The lady with the baby cried and went away.

Then a trickle of men started coming by, and the trickle grew to a stream. Gaunt men, grey men, lame men, men with one eye. And among them some women in the camp found the men they had described as big, strong, golden haired, laughing, and some children found fathers they did not know.

"When will our father come?" my sister and I asked our mother.

"When he comes," our mother said.

The green leaves turned to gold. Then the trees were empty and the snow began creeping down the mountainside. The stream of men dwindled and some of the waiting people's eyes grew empty too, and their hearts grew cold.

But we were the hoping people and every day my sister and I sang our father's songs, and they kept our hearts warm.

"Will our father be here by Christmas?" my sister and I asked our mother.

"Only the good God knows," our mother said, and her face was as thin and pale as birch bark.

The church bell was telling the valley that the Christ Child was coming.

"Let's go and see," I said to my sister.

We climbed the steep path through the Christmas tree forest and tiptoed into the little church. It was calm and sweet and coloured inside. The wind could not find its way in through the thick walls and the candles flamed bright and steady. The sun on the windows bathed us in red and violet and blue. And snug in the corner there was a crib.

Mary and Joseph, the shepherds and the kings were looking down at the baby.

I knelt down to see his face better, and I smiled, because he was smiling at me. "Look!" I said.

But my sister would not smile. She was angry. "It's not fair," she said.

I didn't know what wasn't fair. Was it that the baby was chubby and dimpled and happy, so different from the shrivelled, peevish little ones we had known? Was it that Mary had a beautiful blue dress, so different from our mother's darned black one? Or that Joseph had two arms? Or that the kings had gifts? Or that the cow looked so like ours which the hungry people had eaten?

Before I could ask, my sister had turned away. She grabbed the big brass candlestick and she hit the baby with it. Hard. Harder. Harder still. His little smiling face cracked and his chubby pink arms crumbled into plaster fragments.

My sister let out a big sob and ran from the church.

I ran after her. Calling her name. Begging her to wait for me. But she wouldn't. I tripped over a root and when I got up, she had disappeared.

I hurried back to the camp. I couldn't see her anywhere. But I didn't ask my mother. I took my doll and ran back up into the forest.

The sun had gone down behind the mountain and the trees were dark. I called my sister and sang our father's songs. But the wind gulped down my voice and made the trees moan.

Inside the church the light and colour had almost gone. The candles had almost died. I stole another from the box and lit it before the last one guttered out.

I took off my blouse and knelt down by the crib. Carefully I wrapped the plaster pieces in my blouse and when the space was as clean as I could make it, I laid my doll there.

Just off the path back to the camp I found a hollow under a big tree. I hid my bundle in it and covered it with pine needles.

Back at the camp our mother was hunting for us. "Where have you been?" she asked me. "And where is your sister?" And her voice was as shrill as the wind through the cracks in the walls of our hut.

My sister slipped in like a shadow and my mother did not even notice that my blouse was missing.

The snow came down in the night and in the morning all the valley was white and hushed. Then over the mountainside we could see the first of the searching people for the day arriving, coming down the slope like ants. And suddenly across the snow I could hear a mouth-organ.

"It's Father!" I called.

And I ran. And ran. Shouting. Falling in the snow drifts. Laughing. Crying.

I was the first to reach him. And he hugged me. And hugged me. And hugged me.

Then my sister came. And he hugged her.

And my mother. And they hugged each other.

And we all hugged each other.

Till Father said, "Careful. We don't want to break the other wing". And he pulled something out of his pocket.

I thought it would be a bird—a blue tit or a goldfinch.

But it was a fragment of glass. And in the glass there was an angel. Blue as the sky and gold as the sun.

My sister fingered the sharp edges. "Its wing is broken," she said sadly.

"But look!" I said. "It's playing a mouth-organ!"

"You could say so," Father laughed.

"Where did you find it?" Mother asked.

"In the ruins of a church," Father said. "And it's kept me company all the time I've been searching for you."

"And how did you find us?"

Father laughed again. "Whenever I went into a camp, I played my mouth-organ. And children used to come up to me and say, 'Those are the songs Lena and Anna used to sing. You must be their father. They said you had one arm and played the mouth-organ.' So I knew I'd find you somewhere, some day."

My sister said, "Can we go home now?" And our mother asked it with her eyes.

But our father shook his head. "There's no home to go to. And other people have taken our land."

My sister said, "It's not fair. After everything . . ."

But our father put his mouth-organ to her lips and her words turned into funny sounds. And we all laughed.

"We'll find another home," our father said. "You'll see."

And we did. Though it took a long while . . .

Ingrid put her hand on mine. "And you've put the angel on the Christmas tree ever since."

Peter put his hand on Ingrid's. "You unwrap it. You're more careful than I am."

Ingrid opened the box and picked up the blue and gold angel. It glowed like a star in her hand. "How sad its wing is broken. You put it on the tree, Peter. You're taller than I am."

Peter stretched up with the fragment of glass.

And the little angel with the mouth-organ proclaimed its message from on high once more.

First published in 1984 by Hodder & Stoughton (Australia) Pty Limited,
First American publication 1986 by Holiday House, Inc.
Printed in Hong Kong

Library of Congress Cataloging-in-Publication Data

Mattingley, Christobel.
  The angel with a mouth-organ.

  Summary: Just before the glass angel is put on the
Christmas tree, Mother describes her experiences as a
little girl during World War II when she and her
family were refugees and how the glass angel came to
symbolize a new beginning in their lives.
  [1. World War, 1939-1945 – Fiction. 2. War – Fiction.
3. Christmas – Fiction.] I. Lacis, Astra, ill.
II. Title.
PZ7.M43543An 1986   [E]   85-16424
ISBN 0-8234-0593-1